Martin Wa~~e~~ ~~eh has~~ ~~books fo~~ ~~en~~ of all ages. He also writes under the pen-name of Catherine Sefton. He has won a number of awards including the Smarties Prize twice, the Kurt Maschler Award and was a runner-up for the *Guardian* Children's Fiction Prize. He now lives by the sea in Northern Ireland with his wife, three sons and their dog, Bessie.

THE GHOST FAMILY ROBINSON
THE GHOST FAMILY ROBINSON
  AT THE SEASIDE
HERBIE WHISTLE
THE LUCKY DUCK SONG

In Puffin

NAPPER GOES FOR GOAL
NAPPER STRIKES AGAIN
NAPPER'S GOLDEN GOALS
NAPPER'S BIG MATCH
NAPPER·SUPER-SUB
NAPPER'S LUCK

Picture books

GOING WEST (*with Philippe Dupasquier*)
MAN MOUNTAIN (*with Claudio Muñoz*)

Books by Catherine Sefton

In Young Puffin

THE HAUNTED SCHOOLBAG

In Puffin

ALONG A LONELY ROAD
BERTIE BOGGIN AND THE GHOST AGAIN!
THE GHOST AND BERTIE BOGGIN

THE GHOST FAMILY ROBINSON

Martin Waddell

Illustrated by Jacqui Thomas

PUFFIN BOOKS

PUFFIN BOOKS

Published by the Penguin Group
Penguin Books Ltd, 27 Wrights Lane, London W8 5TZ, England
Penguin Books USA Inc., 375 Hudson Street, New York, New York 10014, USA
Penguin Books Australia Ltd, Ringwood, Victoria, Australia
Penguin Books Canada Ltd, 10 Alcorn Avenue, Toronto, Ontario, Canada M4V 3B2
Penguin Books (NZ) Ltd, 182–190 Wairau Road, Auckland 10, New Zealand

Penguin Books Ltd, Registered Offices: Harmondsworth, Middlesex, England

First published by Viking 1990
Published in Puffin Books 1991
10 9 8 7 6 5

Text copyright © Martin Waddell, 1990
Illustrations copyright © Jacqui Thomas, 1990
All rights reserved

The moral right of the author and illustrator has been asserted

Printed in England by Clays Ltd, St Ives plc
Filmset in Linotron 202 Times

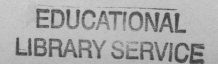

Chapter One

The Ghost Family Robinson live at Mrs Watts' house, where I go after school, so I know more about them than almost anyone.

There are four of them. Mum Robinson is the Mum and Pirate Robinson is the Dad and Harold Robinson is the spotty one (I didn't think ghosts *had* spots until I met Harold, but he has lots) and Hetty Robinson is the my-sized Robinson. We play together when I'm waiting for my Mum to get home from work.

One day Mrs Watts said: "I'm going on holiday this weekend, Tom."

"Where to, Aggie?" I said. Aggie lets me call her Aggie, because she doesn't like being called "Mrs Watts". It makes her feel old and she's only seventy-three.

"To my brother Arthur," she said.

"Can I come too?" I asked.

"Not this time," she said. "It's only for the weekend, and your Mum and Dad will be home."

There was a sort of *shiver* in the air, and one of Aggie's flower vases lifted off the table and floated round the room. Then it went *bump-bump-bump* three times on the mantelpiece.

Aggie didn't notice it. She has funny double-glazed glasses and a hearing aid, so she misses a lot.

Bump-bump-bump went the vase, a second time, and Aggie's football coupon floated up in the air, and frisked around my head.

I knew it was Hetty's Mum,

trying to tell me she was
worried. I couldn't *see* her,
because the Robinsons are like
that. They don't often *let* people
see them (even real friends like
me) but I knew it was Mum
Robinson doing the vase

banging and the football pool floating just the same, because she likes floating vases about, and she doesn't approve of Aggie's football pools.

Mum Robinson must have wisped upstairs and told Pirate what was going on, because the next thing I heard was *thump-thump-thump*, which is the noise Pirate makes when he bangs his wooden leg coming down the stairs.

"Aggie," I said. "You *can't* go on holiday."

"Why not?" said Aggie.

"What will happen to the Robinsons?" I said.

"Your ghosts, Tom?" Aggie

said, with a laugh. "I'm sure your ghosts would like me to have a holiday."

"I'm sure they *wouldn't*," I said.

"You tell your ghosts I'm going just the same," Aggie

said. "I've got my pensioners' weekend return booked already. They'll never miss me."

Bang-bang-bang went the flower vase, hopping up and down on the mantelpiece.

Thump-thump-thump went Pirate's peg-leg, beside Aggie's chair, although she didn't seem to notice it.

Clunk-clink-clunk went the letter-box (that was spotty Harold, who used to be a postman).

ZZZZZ-ZZZZZ-ZZZZZ! The electric light flashed on and off and on again. (Hetty is very good at electrical things. She is the cleverest Robinson, even if she is the smallest ghost.)

"You know the Robinsons don't like being lonely," I said. "They'd be frightened in your house, all on their own."

"I'm sure they'll manage very well without me," she said.

"No they *won't*," I said, and Hetty flashed the lights again, in agreement.

"Well then, we'll have to think of something, won't we?" said Aggie, and she took her teeth out to have a think. Then she put her teeth back in again and said: "Supposing . . . supposing they come *with* me?"

Harold went *clunk-clink-clunk* on the letter-box.

"Harold gets carsick," I said.

"I'm not going by car," Aggie said. "I'm going by train."

Clunk! Bump! ZZZ! Thump! went the Robinsons.

"I don't think the Robinsons like trains," I said. "In fact I don't think they like travelling at all."

"They'll just have to stay here then, won't they?" said Aggie.

Then my Mum came.

"Tom doesn't want me to go

away, Madge," Aggie said.
"He's worried about his
ghosts."

"They're not *my* ghosts," I
said quickly, because the
Robinsons are very easily
offended. "They're the
Robinsons."

My Mum laughed. "I don't
think you should worry too
much about the Robinsons,

Tom," she said. My Mum didn't *believe* in the Robinsons. She thought I was just making them up.

"Well, it would be better if the Robinsons had somewhere to stay while I'm away," Aggie said, and she winked at Mum.

"Oh!" said Mum. "Yes! Right! Message understood!

I've got the perfect answer to the problem of What-To-Do-About-The-Robinsons."

"What?" I said.

"They can come on holiday to our house, while Mrs Watts is away!" said my Mum. "You tell them that, Tom. They're to come across the road to our house."

So I did.

"Hold on!" said Hetty. "We'll
have to have a huddle."

That is what ghosts do, when
they have something to think
over. They huddle up together
and think about it. It keeps
their conversations private,
because they can whisper, and
it keeps them warm.

Hetty came out of the huddle.

"My Mum says that would be nice, so long as your Mum doesn't *mind* having her house haunted."

I told my Mum, and my Mum said: "I don't mind being haunted one bit, Tom, so long as it keeps your Robinsons happy."

"That's the ticket!" said
Aggie, and she laughed so
much she almost swallowed her
teeth.

"Tell the Robinsons we'll
expect them on Friday," my

Mum said when we were going.
"Tell them we're looking
forward to having them."

But I couldn't find any of the
Robinsons to tell.

They must have been upstairs
packing.

Chapter Two

The Robinsons came to our house the next day, which was Friday, after seeing Aggie off.

They came so quietly that no one knew they were there, except me.

My Mum certainly didn't. She walked through spotty Harold *three* times in the hall, and never noticed him.

Harold was upset.

He *clunk-clinked* our letter-box, which was clever of him, because we haven't got a letter-box. I didn't know *how* he had done it, and neither did my Mum.

She was really puzzled.

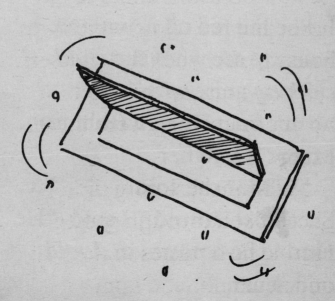

She hunted all round the house to see what the *clunk-clinking* noise was.

"It's only Harold Robinson, Mum," I told her.

"Who?" she said.

"*Ghost* Harold," I said. "He used to be a postman. I *told* you, Mum."

"Oh!" she said. "Yes. I see! That would explain it!" I don't think that she really believed me, because I heard her scolding my Dad about the noisy central heating.

There wasn't much haunting apart from that, just a few *chills* on the landing and some whiffs of Pirate's pipe smoke in the bathroom and a bit of flickering on the TV set because Hetty got bored with the programmes.

Then our cat sat on her, or tried to. I think our cat could *see* Hetty, but of course when she sat on Hetty's knee, she went *through* it, and ended up on the cushion.

Hetty got up and went out.

The cat sat there twitching its tail and looking puzzled.

I went after Hetty.

She was out in the back garden, in my tree house.

"Hullo, Hetty," I said.

"Hullo," she said.

She was looking gloomy.

"What's the matter?" I said.

"*Being good* is the matter," she said. "My Mum says we are visitors here and we have to behave ourselves, and it isn't interesting, that's all. I'm bored."

"What do you *want* to do?" I said.

"One of my special haunts," she said. "I think that would be really interesting. An exciting one like . . . like . . ."

". . . like the Headless Horseman in the Ghost Book Aggie gave me for Christmas?" I said.

"What did he do?" Hetty asked, sounding interested. She likes books about ghosts because she *is* a ghost herself.

"Galloped up and down the road with no head on," I said.

Hetty thought a bit.

"Trouble is, I've *got* a head," she said.

"And you haven't got a
horse," I said.

"No Headless Horseman,
then," she said. "What other
ghosts were there in your book?"

"There was Anne Boleyn," I
said. "She got her head cut off

34

and walks the Bloody Tower looking for it."

"Don't you know about any ghosts who've kept their heads *on*?" she said.

"Most ghosts I know about have their heads off," I said.

"I don't," said Hetty. "And Mum doesn't. And Dad doesn't. Neither does spotty Harold."

"Ghosts in books, I mean," I said.

"We are real ghosts," she said. "I'm fed up. I'm going drift-about," and she glided off down the garden, and straight through the back wall of our house.

I should have done something about it, to stop Hetty being bored. I should have played hopscotch with her, or some game like that. Hetty is good at hopscotch. Most ghosts are, because they don't weigh very

much, and don't hurt themselves if they fall over.

Hopscotch might have stopped her, but I didn't think of it.

I stayed there wondering if *being good* for more than a day was *possible*, for a ghost like Hetty.

Chapter Three

Saturday morning was all right, nothing much happened. I think Hetty must have been drifting about somewhere, having a ghost-think.

On Saturday afternoon, Hetty started moving things. Just small things, like my Dad's magazine, or my Mum's screwdriver.

She floated my Mum's

screwdriver all the way round
the kitchen, and then dropped it
back on the table.

"What was that?" my Mum
said.

"Hetty was playing with your
screwdriver, Mum," I said.

"Oh, yes?" she said. "Hetty,
was it?"

My Mum thought that it was
me!

Then Hetty did some walking
about.

Tap-tap-tap went her feet across the ceiling. My Dad went upstairs to see what was doing the tapping, and the tapping stopped.

My Dad came downstairs, grumbling.

Tap-tap-tap again, as soon as he sat down.

Mum went upstairs this time.

The tapping stopped.

Mum came down, shaking her head, then . . .

Tap-tap-tap again.

"What's making that noise?" Dad said.

"Hetty," I said.

"*Who?*" said Dad.

"Hetty Ghost-Robinson!" my Mum said, and she winked at him. "One of Tom's ghosts!"

"Ghosts!" harrumphed my Dad, and he went back to reading his paper.

Behind him, a cushion floated up in the air, waved

about, and dropped down again.
I don't think Hetty was pleased.

She didn't do anything until
after tea-time, when I was up in
my room.

Bang! went something on
the stairs.

We dashed to see what it was,

but there was nothing there.

"I'm beginning to think this place really is haunted!" said my Mum.

"How did you do that bang?" I asked Hetty, when she came drifting through my bedroom wall afterwards.

"I'm very good at bangs," Hetty said. "But I'm very cross with your Mum. What does she mean saying: *'I'm beginning to think this place really is haunted'?*"

I didn't say anything.

"If I wasn't being *good* I could show her some *real* haunting," Hetty said.

"You're only boasting," I said.

"Say that again!" said Hetty, shimmering slightly.

"Boasting," I said. "You don't do real haunts at all, not like the ghosts in my book."

"Oh, don't we?" said Hetty. "You wait and see, Tom Potts.

Just you wait and see!"

And she disappeared.

Nothing happened for ages and ages, until we'd all gone to bed, and then . . .

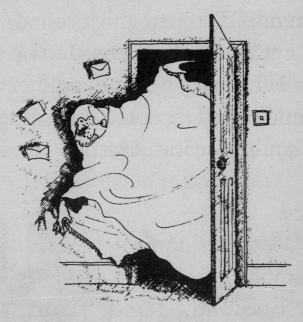

. . . my door creaked open, and a spotty, ghostly figure wrapped in a sheet drifted into my room.

"OAAAH! OOOOOOH!"
it moaned.

"Hullo, Harold," I said.

"It's not me," said Harold
Robinson, indignantly. "I'm a
dreadfully scary ghost called
. . . what am I supposed to be
called, Hetty?" Hetty put her
head round the door and said:
"You're useless, Harold!" and

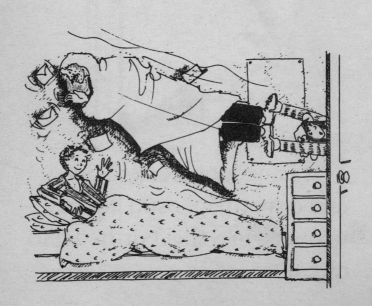

they both disappeared.

"Harold!" I shouted.
"Hetty!"

I shouldn't have shouted. I'd forgotten about Mum and Dad.

They both came running into my bedroom. My Mum had a poker for banging burglars with.

"What's happened?" my Dad said, switching on the light.

"Oh – er . . . nothing," I said. "It was just the Robinsons."

"That's it!" Mum said. "This Ghost-Robinson-Pretend-Game has gone on long enough, Tom. It has to stop."

"There are no Robinsons, Tom," said Dad, firmly. "They are just a silly game that Mrs Watts made up to keep you happy when you are in her house after school. I wish she hadn't bothered."

"The Robinsons are real!" I said.

But they wouldn't believe me. The Robinsons must have

heard my Mum and Dad telling
me off. They came floating
through the wall the minute my
Mum and Dad left the room.

The Robinsons were very cross.

"Not believing in people is *rude*!" Mum Robinson said.

"I've never ever not been believed in before!" said Pirate.

"They don't mean to be rude," I said.

"How would you like it if *we*

didn't believe in *you*?" Hetty said.

"That's different!" I said.

"Oh it is, is it?" said Hetty. "So we are not *real*, and your Mum and Dad are quite right not to believe in us! We'll soon see about that!"

"You tell him, Hetty!" said spotty Harold.

"This is what comes of *being good*!" said Hetty. "From now on, we're haunting this house the way it ought to be haunted!"

"For the sake of the family honour!" said Pirate.

"One for all and all for one!" said spotty Harold.

"I agree!" said Mum Robinson.

And then they all vanished.

The lights went on and off three times, ZZZ-ZZZ-ZZZ, and the curtains gave an angry flutter, but that was all.

"I believe in you Hetty," I said, to the space where Hetty had been, but I don't think she heard me. I don't think it would have made any difference anyway.

The Robinsons wanted to prove to my Mum and Dad that they were real ghosts. I just didn't know how they would set about doing it.

Chapter Four

Sunday began very quietly.

It was as if the Robinsons had gone on strike, or gone back over the road to Aggie's house, but they hadn't. I knew that they hadn't because I heard,

Pieces of eight!

Pieces of eight!

It was coming from Pirate's parrot (I forgot to say it was a talking parrot, as well as being a ghost parrot). That was when I was upstairs in the bathroom, and then I walked *through* two chills in the hall.

Apart from that, I didn't notice anything ghostly at all.

My Mum said, "I'm glad to see you are behaving yourself

today, Tom, with no more of your Ghost-Robinson nonsense."

I expect the Robinsons were resting, or maybe they had decided to take the morning off to think things over, or they'd gone drift-about.

Sunday afternoon was different.

It began about half past two, when the front doorbell rang.

BRRRRRRRRRRRRRRRR-RRNG!

"Go and see who that is, Tom," Mum said.

I opened the front door to see who was there, but nobody was.

So I closed the door again.

BRNNNNNNG! BRNNNNNG!

BRRRRRRRNNNNGGGG!

I opened the door again.

Nobody was there *again*.

I closed it.

**BRRRRRRRRRNNNNNG!
BRNNNNG! BRRRRRRRNG!
BRRRRRRRRRRRRRRNNNN-
NNNNNGGGGG!**

"Tom! Stop playing games!"
my Mum shouted, coming down
the stairs.

Then . . .

*BONG-BONG-BONG-
BONG-BONG.* Somebody
started beating the old bongo
drums that my Dad keeps under
the bed, and at the same time
the TV and Dad's clock radio
upstairs and Mum's radio in the

kitchen and the washing
machine and the hairdryer and
the record player all started
working at once
and
all the taps in the house started
running

and
the flower vases and pictures
started moving about, all on
their own, flying from room to
room
and
so did the cushions

and

our clothes came out of their
drawers and flew up and down
the stairs

and

my Dad's harmonica started
playing all by itself in mid-air in
the back room

and
three eggs hopped out of the
egg rack and did a roll around
the kitchen
and
the pots and pans came out of
their cupboard and clattered up
on top of each other in the sink
and
the brushes and the dusters

chased the hoover up and down
the hall
and
all the curtains started flapping
and fluttering
and

all our lights were swinging
about, as well as ZZZZZZ-ing
on and off.

"Help!" screeched Mum,
grabbing me and making for
the door.

"Wait for me!" shouted Dad, and he came after us, dodging two cushions and a pillow which came flying down the stairs.

We got out into our garden at the front and stood on the bench, where the mower couldn't get at us as it whizzed up and down. Not that it was trying to get at us . . . it was too busy chasing the milk bottles that were jigging about on the grass.

"What's happening?" gasped Dad.

"I don't know!" stuttered Mum.

"It's the Robinsons!" I said.

Mum looked at Dad.

"The ROBINSONS?" Dad gasped.

"But we don't *believe* in the Robinsons!" my Mum said.

By this time all the neighbours had heard the noise

and they came out into the
street to see our funny house,
with the lights flashing on and
off and the curtains fluttering
and the doorbell ringing and
my Dad's bongo drums
bongo-ing and the radios and
the TV and record player
playing and the cushions flying
about.

"Is that *why* there is all this

fuss?" asked my Dad. "Because we don't believe in the Robinsons?"

"Yes," I said. "Hetty was really angry about it."

My Mum looked at my Dad

and my Dad looked at my Mum
and then they both looked at
me and then:
   "I BELIEVE IN THE
ROBINSONS!" my Dad shouted
   and
   "I DO TOO!" my Mum shouted
   and

EVERYTHING STOPPED.

There wasn't a sound.

"I told you," I said.

"Phew!" said my Dad.

"I'm glad that that is all over," said my Mum weakly.

The neighbours came in wanting to know what the trouble was and asking questions and saying What-A-Thing-To-Happen-In-Our-Street and went on about the mess.

They tramped over everything and made things worse, and it was ages and ages before we could get them to go away. My Dad told them it was a small earthquake, limited to our house, but I don't think that they believed him.

We went back into the house.

"Is that . . .?" my Mum gasped, suddenly.

"Mrs Robinson," I said. "The one putting things straight in the kitchen."

"Who's *that*?" my Dad said.

"The one with the parrot and the wooden leg?" I said. "That's Mr Robinson. He's called Pirate because he used to be one." Pirate Robinson was putting the cushions back on the chairs.

"And the little one cleaning

up the stairs?" my Mum stuttered. "That's . . . that's . . .?"

"That's Hetty," I said. "She's my special friend. And Harold is the one who is putting all the pictures straight."

"I should have known it was Harold because of the spots," my Mum said.

"Yes," my Dad said. "Tom told us about the spots."

"Don't say anything to Harold about them," I said. "He doesn't much like being spotty."

My Mum went into the kitchen and made us all a cup of tea . . . us and the Robinsons, though I couldn't work out where the tea *went* when the Robinsons drank it. It sort of *disappeared* inside them.

My Dad got his bongo drums out from under the bed and showed Harold and Pirate how to play them properly and I was busy explaining how our TV

goes wonky to Hetty when . . .

BRRRNG! BRNNNG!

It was Aggie Watts.

"I'm back!" she said. "I couldn't stay long in Arthur's house. He's so *old*, and it's so quiet."

"Did you miss having the Robinsons about the place?" my Mum said.

"*Who?*" said Aggie. "Oh . . . *yes*, the *Robinsons*. Your Tom's ghosts."

"They're *our* ghosts now," said my Mum.

"Of course I missed them," said Aggie, and she winked at my Mum and cackled.

The Robinsons went back

across the road with Aggie to
her house, although it took
them ages to finish moving back
all the things from our roof
space.

"You know, Tom," my Mum
said. "I believe in the
Robinsons, and your Dad
believes in the Robinsons, and

you believe in the Robinsons, but I don't think Mrs Watts does, do you?"

"She thinks they are a pretend game I play in her house," I said.

My Mum thought about it.

"I don't think we should tell the Robinsons that Mrs Watts doesn't believe in them, Tom," she said. "Do you?"